SPONGEBOB SQUAREPANTS

FIVE
Undersea Stories

created by

Stephen Hillenburg

Visit us on the Web!
StepIntoReading.com
randomhousekids.com

Educators and librarians, for a variety of teaching tools, visit us at RHTeachersLibrarians.com

ISBN 978-0-553-50860-4

MANUFACTURED IN CHINA   10 9 8 7 6 5 4 3 2

nickelodeon

SpongeBob
SQUAREPANTS™

FIVE
Undersea Stories

A Collection of Five
Step 2 Early Readers

Random House 🏠 New York

Contents

STEP INTO READING®

2

STEP

READING WITH HELP

DANCING WITH THE STAR

By Alex Harvey
Illustrated by Stephen Reed

Random House 🏠 New York

Pearl watches TV.
Her favorite show
is a dance contest.

12

Mr. Krabs sees the host.

The host is his friend!

Pearl wants to have

a dance contest

with the host!

Mr. Krabs invites
his friend.
He can host the contest.
It will be at the
Krusty Krab.

SpongeBob and
Squidward
are very excited.

Squidward wants to win the contest!

18

SpongeBob and
Squidward
hang flyers
all over town.

Sandy wants to win
with the Texas two-step.

Larry the Lobster
practices
the cha-cha.

Patrick wants to enter
the contest.
But he is scared.

SpongeBob decides
to help his friend.

Patrick and SpongeBob
go to SpongeBob's house.

SpongeBob puts on music.
Patrick twists.

He flops.

He falls on his face!

Patrick needs help.

SpongeBob will train
Patrick!

SpongeBob helps Patrick.

Patrick runs.

He sweats.

He learns ballet.

He dances!

The contest begins.
Everyone is
at the Krusty Krab.

The cameras roll.

The host

greets the crowd.

The judges are ready!

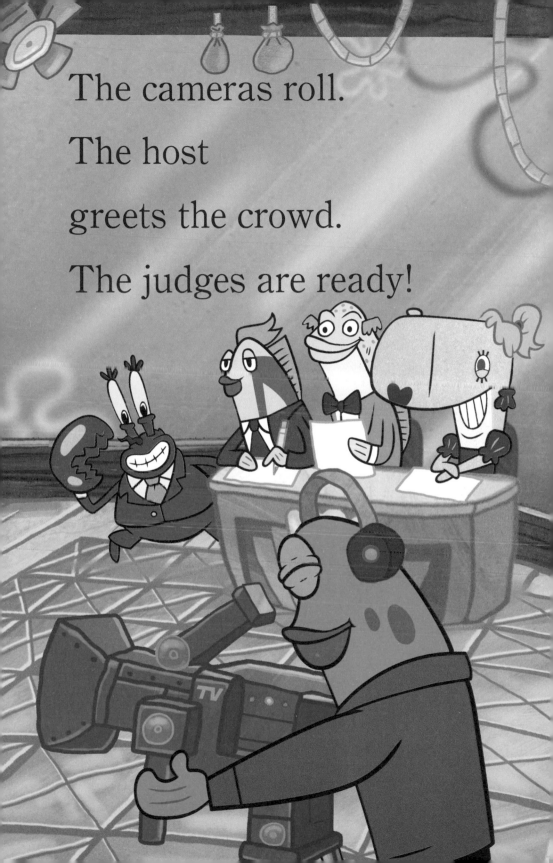

Squidward goes first.

He twirls.

He gets tangled up!

Sandy is next.

She dances.

She is great!

Larry does the cha-cha.

He is very good.

It is Patrick's turn.

He is nervous.

SpongeBob gives Patrick

the thumbs-up!

Patrick starts.

He boogies.

He flips

across the floor.

Patrick is the best!

He wins the contest!

Patrick is a dance star!

He really likes to cook
Krabby Patties!

Mr. Krabs wants
to save money.
He fires
SpongeBob!

SpongeBob walks home.

He is very sad.

SpongeBob wants
a new job.

He goes to Weenie Hut.

He gets a new job.

Instead of hot dogs,
SpongeBob makes
Weenie Patties.
The boss is not happy.

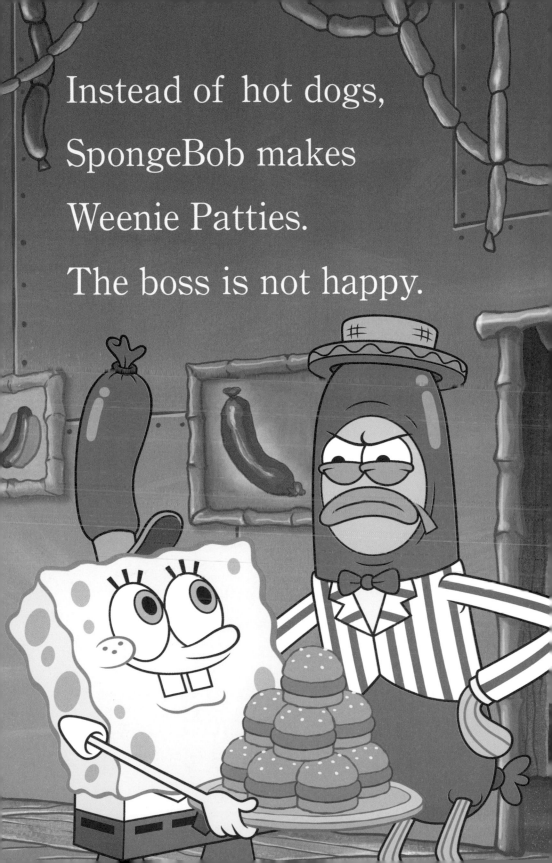

SpongeBob loses
the Weenie Hut job.

SpongeBob gets
a job at the Pizza Piehole.
But he does not make
normal pizzas.

The boss does not like SpongeBob's Pizza Patties.

SpongeBob loses
his job again.

53

Back at home,
SpongeBob makes
dinner for Gary.
"You still like my cooking,"
says SpongeBob.

Knock! Knock!

A giant hot dog grabs SpongeBob!

The customers love the Weenie Patties! SpongeBob is forced to make more.

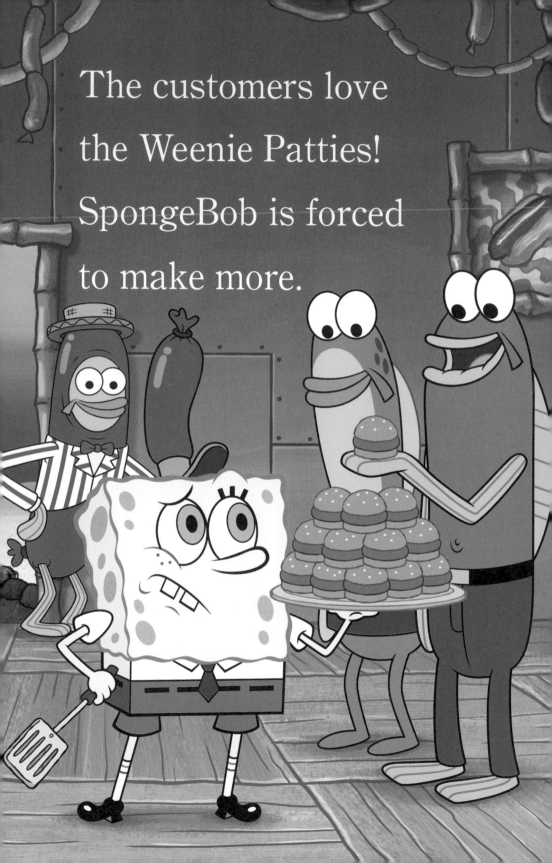

The Pizza Piehole wants
SpongeBob back, too.
People love
his Pizza Patties!

Now everyone wants
SpongeBob!

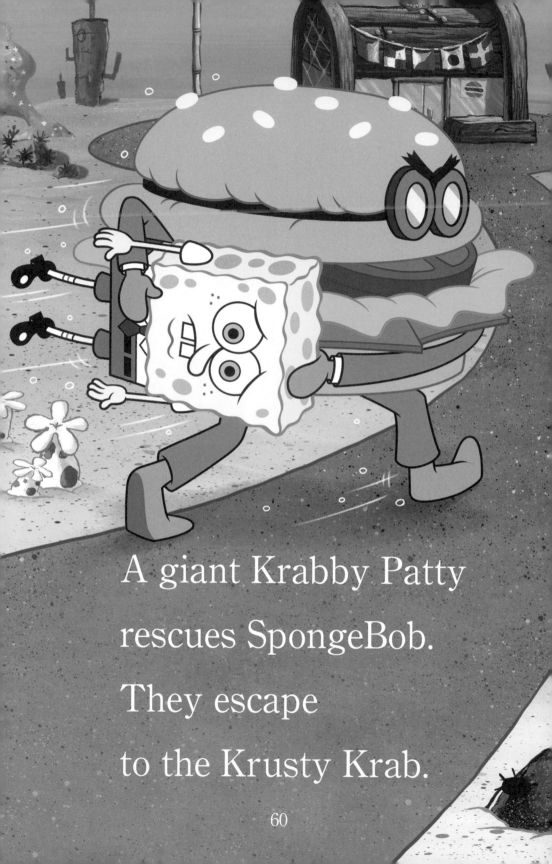

A giant Krabby Patty
rescues SpongeBob.
They escape
to the Krusty Krab.

The Krabby Patty is really Squidward!

The Krusty Krab is
a mess without
SpongeBob.

"Please work for me again," begs Mr. Krabs.

SpongeBob is happy
to work
at the Krusty Krab again!

Party Time!

By John Cabell

Illustrated by Harry Moore

Random House 🏠 New York

It is
Squidward's birthday!
He gives himself
a new clarinet.

Squidward goes outside.
He plays
his new clarinet.

SpongeBob
is also outside.
He plays fetch
with Gary.

SpongeBob throws
a stick.
"Go get it, Gary!"
he says.

Gary brings

the stick back.

"Meow," says Gary.

72

Squidward puts
the clarinet down.

Oh, no!
SpongeBob accidentally
grabs the clarinet
and throws it.

Crack!

The clarinet breaks.

"I'm sorry,"

says SpongeBob.

"You have ruined my birthday!" yells Squidward.

SpongeBob must fix
Squidward's birthday.
"I will throw him
the best party ever,"
he says.

Patrick will help.

The party will be

at the Krusty Krab.

SpongeBob makes

a delicious cake.

Patrick blows
up balloons
and decorates
the Krusty Krab.

SpongeBob and Patrick make a giant ice statue of Squidward.

SpongeBob wraps
a special gift
for Squidward.
Everything is ready
for the party!

83

Mr. Krabs goes
to Squidward's house.
<u>Knock, knock!</u>

Squidward opens
the door.
"There is an emergency
at the Krusty Krab!"
says Mr. Krabs.

Squidward and Mr. Krabs
run to the Krusty Krab.

When Squidward
walks in,
everyone cheers.
"Surprise!" they shout.

"We are all here to wish you a happy birthday," says SpongeBob.

"I'm here for a Krabby Patty," says a customer.

SpongeBob gives
Squidward a gift.

90

It is

a new clarinet!

Squidward plays a song.

Hooray!
Everyone claps.
Squidward bows.

Squidward thanks
SpongeBob.
"This was
a great birthday,"
he says.

Happy birthday,
Squidward!

Moms
Are the Best!

By Sarah Wilson

Illustrated by Dave Aikins

Random House 🏠 New York

SpongeBob
is late for work.
He had to mail
an essay
to the Best Mom Contest.

Mr. Krabs gets
an idea.

"The Krusty Krab will have a special day for moms!" he says.

Mr. Krabs thinks
his plan will make him
lots of money!

Squidward calls
his mom.

SpongeBob calls
his mom.

It's the big day!

The Krusty Krab is full
of mothers and children.

Ring!

SpongeBob gets
a phone call.
It's his mother.

There is a leak
in her house.
She can't attend the lunch.

SpongeBob is sad.

Everybody's mom is there—

except his.

Squidward's mom
doesn't like
the Krusty Krab.

"Who can I complain to?"

she asks.

"Where is your mom?"
Mr. Krabs asks
SpongeBob.

SpongeBob quickly thinks of an answer.

"My mom is a star,"
SpongeBob says.
"She has to go
someplace fancy
in her big car."

No one believes
SpongeBob.

The leak is fixed!
Now SpongeBob's mom
can go to the
Krusty Krab!

SpongeBob's essay
wins the contest!
His mother really is
a star—for a day!

SpongeBob's mom can do
anything she wants.
"I want to eat
at the Krusty Krab,"
she says.

She gets into
a big, fancy car.

At the Krusty Krab,

SpongeBob is sad.

"Too bad your mom
can't drive here
in her big car,"
Squidward says.

123

Suddenly,
a big car arrives.
SpongeBob's mom is
in it!

SpongeBob runs
to her.

Cameras flash.
People cheer.
Squidward can't believe
his eyes.

SpongeBob and
his mother
eat lunch.
"Moms are the best!"
he says.

The Great Train Mystery

Adapted by David Lewman

Illustrated by The Artifact Group

Based on the screenplay "Krabby Patty No More" by Casey Alexander, Zeus Cervas, Steven Banks, and Dani Michaeli

Random House 🏠 New York

Mr. Krabs needs a recipe.

It is in a locked box.

Mr. Krabs gives

SpongeBob

the key to the box.

SpongeBob and Patrick
will get the recipe.
They take a train.

Plankton is
on the train.
He wants the key.

SpongeBob and Patrick
are very hungry.
They go to the dining car.

SpongeBob and Patrick
meet a nanny
and her baby.

SpongeBob meets
a porter.
The porter does not like
SpongeBob.

He pushes SpongeBob

off his seat!

SpongeBob and Patrick
leave the dining car.
They want to hide
the key.

The key is gone!
SpongeBob cannot
find it!

SpongeBob sees
Plankton.
He thinks Plankton
stole the key!

Patrick checks Plankton.
Plankton does not have
the key.

Patrick lets Plankton go.
SpongeBob asks Patrick
to call the cops.

Patrick shouts
for the cops.

The cops arrive.
SpongeBob tells them
about the missing key.

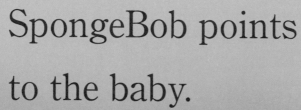

SpongeBob points
to the baby.

"The baby has the key,"
SpongeBob says.

SpongeBob points
to the nanny.
"She stole the key!"
he says.

SpongeBob holds
the baby.
The police chief
searches the baby.

He finds a stolen jewel!

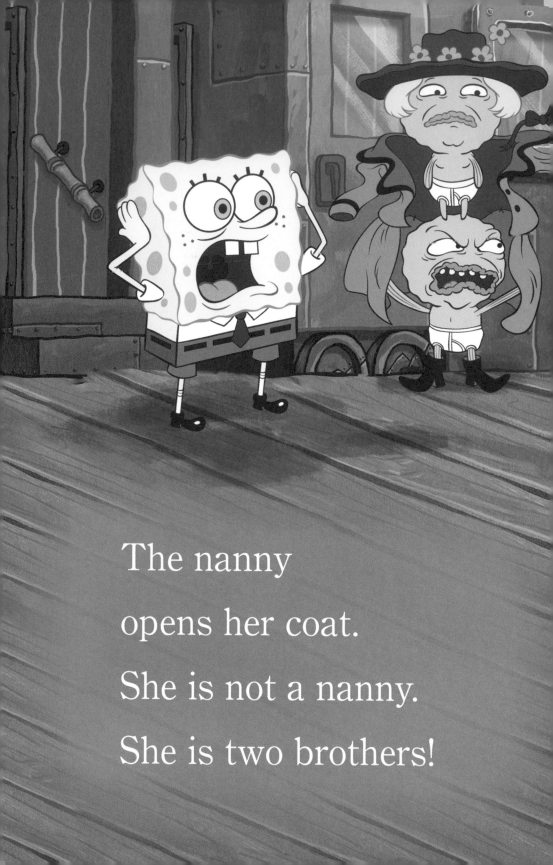

The nanny
opens her coat.
She is not a nanny.
She is two brothers!

SpongeBob has found
the Jewel Triplets Gang!
But he has not found
the missing key.

SpongeBob thinks
the porter stole the key.
Plankton wants the key.
He jumps on the porter.

A policeman shakes
the porter.
A stapler, a hammer,
and an anvil fall out!

A mask falls off the porter.

He is really
a ham sandwich thief!
But SpongeBob still
has not found the key.

Wait!

Patrick has something.

It is the key!

He gives SpongeBob
the key.

SpongeBob and Patrick
solve the mystery!
Now they can get
the recipe.
Plankton is
right behind them.